W9-BNT-644

First published in the United States in 1989 by Chronicle Books.

First published by Libroport Co., Ltd., Tokyo, Japan.

Printed in Hong Kong.

Library of Congress Cataloging-in-Publication Data

Gomi, Taro.
Spring is here / text and pictures by Taro Gomi.
32p. 20 x 25.4cm.
Summary: Text and pictures take us through a year of seasons beginning when spring arrives and a calf is born.
ISBN 0-8118-1022-4 (pb.)
ISBN 0-87701-626-7 (hc.)
(1. Seasons—Fiction.) I. Title.
PZ7.G585Cal 1989
(E)—dc19
88-39848

CIP

AC

Distributed in Canada by Raincoast Books
9050 Shaughnessy Street, Vancouver, British Columbia V6P 6E5

10 9 8 7 6 5 4 3

Chronicle Books LLC
85 Second Street, San Francisco, California 94105

www.chroniclebooks.com

Spring is Here

Taro Gomi

chronicle books
San Francisco

Spring is here.

The snow melts.

The earth is fresh.

The grass sprouts.

The flowers bloom.

The grass grows.

The winds blow.

The storms rage.

The quiet harvest arrives.

The snow falls.

The children play.

The world is hushed.

The world is white.

The snow melts.

The calf has grown.

Spring is here.